The Kid Detective's Handbook

by William Vivian Butler

Illustrated by Sue Dennen

Little, Brown and Company

Boston • New York • Toronto • London

To Mary with all my love
— Bill

For Paul
— Sue

Second Edition

ISBN 0-316-19951-6
Library of Congress Catalog Card Number 94-78896

10 9 8 7 6 5 4 3 2 1

Published simultaneously in Canada
by Little, Brown & Company (Canada) Limited
and in Great Britain by Little, Brown and Company (UK) Limited

Printed in the United States of America

Contents

Whodunit?

Hands Up!

Special Delivery

The Perfect Crime

Stop Right There!

Case Closed

Introduction

Have you ever wondered how famous fictional detectives such as Sherlock Holmes, Nancy Drew, the Hardy Boys, Encyclopedia Brown, and Miss Marple solve their cases? They notice things—often tiny, seemingly unimportant things—that other people miss. And that's an ability they share with the best real-life detectives all over the world.

Whether you ask the FBI or Scotland Yard, they'll tell you the same thing. In the end, it isn't *guns* that beat criminals. It's *brains*—the ability to spot clues, follow them, analyze them, and catch the culprit. If you wish you could develop this ability, *The Kid Detective's Handbook and Scene-of-the-Crime Kit* gives you all the tips and tools you need to follow the footsteps—or footprints!— of the great detectives of fiction and fact.

In this book, you can discover how to play a real part in fighting crime—what to watch out for and what to report to the police—as well as how to have fun with detection—including how to start a detective club, test your observation skills, take fingerprints, collect clues, make deductions, send secret messages, invent and decipher codes, and even make your own burglar alarm.

Of course, if you come up against any kind of real-life

crime—in school or in your neighborhood—don't make any attempt to investigate. Just observe, and if it's serious enough, report it. Remember these three important rules of thumb: (1) Keep your eyes open. (2) Write down the exact details of anything suspicious. (3) Get your parents to call the police—or in an emergency, contact the police yourself—but only if you really believe you're on to something important. The police don't have any time to waste!

Kid Detective Helps Crack Case!

An eight-year-old girl noticed some suspicious activity in her neighborhood in London—three men had been sitting in a car in the same place for the past half hour. She went to the local police station, produced her notebook, and told the police officer what she had seen, including: (1) the exact place where the car was parked, (2) the make and color of the car, and (3) the license plate number. The police officer called Scotland Yard and read out the details the girl had given him. The information was entered into the national police computer. Within seconds, the computer identified the car as a stolen vehicle. The officer then contacted the inspector in charge of the police station, and soon two police cars rushed to the spot where the little girl had said the car was waiting. The spot turned out to be across the street from a bank to which a large amount of cash was due to be delivered. The men sitting in the car were taken completely by surprise. Before they realized what was happening, they found themselves surrounded by police officers and under arrest! There is no doubt that if the police hadn't arrived when they did, a serious holdup would have taken place; thousands of dollars would have been stolen, and very possibly several people injured or killed. All this was prevented because an eight-year-old girl used her eyes, took care to get all the important facts, and reported them promptly.

You never know when or where you might suddenly find yourself witnessing something suspicious. Just walking down the street, looking out of your bedroom window, or playing in the playground at school—it could happen anywhere. A car racing down the road at a dangerous speed could be a crook escaping after committing a crime. An unfamiliar car in your neighborhood may have been abandoned by a criminal. So keep your eyes and ears alert and practice the activities in this book. Then you'll be ready in case a real crime ever does occur before your very eyes! In the meantime, you can have fun testing your detective skills with your friends and family.

Your Scene-of-the-Crime Kit

This kit is essential for practicing your detection skills. Real-life investigations always begin with a close examination of the scene of the crime. And just as a doctor carries a little black bag containing a stethoscope, thermometer, and other medical equipment, so a detective takes a scene-of-the-crime kit with him to every inquiry. Your kit is based on the one most police experts use. It includes:

Notebook and pencil: to take notes, record observations, and send secret messages to your fellow detectives. The graphite from your pencil also serves as fingerprint powder.

Magnifying glass: the detective's trademark—invaluable for examining anything from a scratch to a thumbprint.

Ink stamp pad: you can use this to create a file of your friends' and family's fingerprints.

Chalk: for drawing arrows at clues and outlining crime areas. You may also grind this up into a powder and use it to lift fingerprints off dark surfaces.

Paintbrush: for applying fingerprint powder with a light touch.

Ruler: for measuring clues and crime areas.

I.D. Card: Show this when you're investigating a case.

In addition, you may want to include a few items that can be easily found in most households:

Tweezers: for picking up small clues, such as hairs or particles of fabric.

Transparent tape: for lifting fingerprints.

Envelopes or small plastic bags: for storing taped fingerprints and other clues.

Flashlight: in case you need to look for clues under ledges or in dark corners.

Watch, clock, or timer: Some of the activities in this book require someone to keep time. If you don't have a timepiece available, you can always just count.

Be sure to bring this kit with you everywhere you go. Remember every good detective's motto: "Be prepared."

Form Your Own Kid Detectives Club

Do you have friends who also want to become super-sleuths? If so, get them together and form your very own Kid Detectives Club (KDC)! Many of the activities and games in this kit can be done alone or with members of your family, but you will have even more fun if you share them with a group. Remember, there's strength in numbers! Here are some tips for your KDC:

- Each member must pledge to fight crime and to help protect his fellow members.

- Choose a meeting place that's safe, secret, and convenient for all the members to get to.

- Invent a password to make sure no one infiltrates your meetings.

- Meet once a week to compare notes.

- Keep a file of suspicious characters.

Keep Your Eyes and Ears Open

Developing Your Powers of Observation

Detectives have to be very observant. This means they have to notice and remember every little detail that ordinary people would miss. This ability helps them recognize suspicious behavior and find important clues at the scene of the crime. Here are some activities to help you develop your powers of observation:

The Key Witness Game

Get together with the members of your KDC and go to a public place, such as a mall, street corner, park, or post office—anywhere there are people. Choose one member to be the leader. The leader times the group for three minutes (or counts to a hundred if she doesn't have a watch) and writes down in her detective notebook descriptions of all the people she sees: what they look like, what they're wearing, and what they're doing. The rest of the members use this time to observe the same scene but are not allowed to write anything down. After the time is up, return to your usual meeting spot and wait another ten minutes. Then all the members except the leader should write down descriptions of everyone they saw. The leader checks her notes to see which player remembers the most people correctly. The member with the most accurate descriptions wins: she is the one who would be able to serve as a key witness in a trial for any real crime, because her observations would be the most reliable.

Detective Dictionary

Memorize these words so you'll sound like a true expert when you investigate your crime.

alibi: a form of defense whereby a defendant tries to prove that he or she was elsewhere when the crime in question was committed.

case: a situation requiring investigation.

clue: a guide to a solution of a problem, mystery, or crime.

deduction: the drawing of a conclusion by reasoning.

evidence: the data on which a conclusion or judgment may be based. The documentary or verbal statements and material objects admissible as testimony in a court of law.

incriminate: to involve in or charge with a wrongful act, as a crime.

lead: information of possible use in a search.

suspect: a person who is thought to have committed a crime.

testimony: a declaration or affirmation of truth or fact, as that given before a court.

witness: one who has seen or head something; may be called to testify before a court to affirm information regarding a crime.

The Spot-the-Difference Game

Choose one member to be the leader. The leader finds
about twenty objects from around the house—such as a
pen, book, glass, comb, and salt shaker—and lays most of
them on a table or on the floor, setting some aside for the
moment. The other members look at the items and try to
remember each one while the leader times them for one
minute (or counts to twenty). Then the members leave
the room (or just turn their backs) while the leader takes
some things away and adds new things. The leader makes
a list in his detective notebook of the items he removes
and of the new items he adds. The members look at the
new spread and try to spot the differences. Each one then
makes his own list of the missing and added items as best
he can. The leader reads out his list, and everyone compares notes. This game tests not only your powers of
observation but your memory as well. If anything was
ever stolen from your room, you'd have a better chance of
noticing it if you had a clear idea in your mind of all the
items that had been in it before, right?

I Spy

You can practice your powers of observation anytime, anywhere—at home, at friends' houses, or even at a doctor's office. Just look around you carefully, ask yourself questions about the place you're in, and think about what the answers tell you about the inhabitant. Are there pictures on the wall? What kinds of books or magazines do you see? A dog dish or litter box indicates the person has a pet. Trophies and award certificates on a shelf can tell you what kinds of things the person does in his free time. An ashtray suggests the person smokes. Look around your own room — what would it tell a detective about *you*?

Be a Backyard Detective

Look around your backyard, your driveway, or around a park, field, or woods nearby. Can you spot any signs that animals have been in the area? Get out your magnifying glass and be on the lookout for these telltale signs:

- Cats like to walk on cars. If a car is dusty, you may see tiny pawprints on it.

- After it snows, look for fresh tracks. Where do they lead?

- Check for tiny bites in the leaves; they'll tell you if a rabbit or other small animal has been nibbling on your plants! Also check for tooth marks on branches or hair sticking to a bush, where it might have scraped off when an animal walked by.

- Take a close look at a spider's web: Has the web been disturbed by people or animals bumping into it?

- A small hole in an apple probably means there was (or is!) a worm in it.

- Listen for unusual sounds at night. A clanging noise, for instance, may mean raccoons or other animals are getting into your garbage cans.

- Look up! A bunch of twigs, leaves, and grass arranged on a tree branch suggests a bird is building its nest there.

- Look down! Holes in the ground, especially underneath bushes or trees, may be homes for rabbits or moles. Tiny hills made of dirt or sand are probably anthills. If you look closely (use your magnifying glass), you may see the ants marching in and out of the opening at the top, sometimes carrying crumbs of food.

- If there are deer in the area, the lower branches of trees (including leaves, twigs, or bark) will be eaten away up to the height of the deer's reach.

- Scratch marks at the bottom of a door might mean a dog or cat lives in the house and scratches the door to let the owner know they want to get in.

Dog

Cat

Bird

Rabbit

Chipmunk

Squirrel

Horse

Human

Innocent Until Proven Guilty

Making Deductions

When Sherlock Holmes's sidekick, Mr. Watson, would ask him how he managed to come to his clever conclusions about a case, Holmes's famous response was:

Elementary, my dear Watson.

The habit of deduction—drawing conclusions from observations—is the sign of a smart detective. But you probably didn't realize that you make simple deductions every day. For example, when you turn on a lamp and it fails to light up, what might you deduce? (1) The lamp is unplugged, (2) the bulb has burned out, or (3) there's been a power failure.

Test Your Wits

Suppose you found a bag in the street. Inside it are two envelopes, both containing letters. Envelope number one has a stamp; is postmarked Denver, Colorado; and has been slit open at the top. It is addressed to:

Terry Brown
13 Nowhere Ave.
San Francisco, California

Envelope number two also has a stamp, but it is not postmarked and has not been opened. It is addressed to:

Ms. Susan Yang
37 Nothing Street
Denver, Colorado

Who would you deduce to be the owner of the bag?

Answer: Envelope number one was opened, which suggests it was sent to the owner. Since envelope number two didn't carry a postmark but does have a stamp, it was obviously destined for the mailbox and therefore must have been written *by*, not *to*, the bag's owner. So Terry Brown is the correct answer.

Collecting and Analyzing Clues

Think about all the things you might find in a wallet, handbag, or coat. What do you suppose are the four greatest aids to deducing facts about the owner? Expert detectives would say:

1. *Letters:* These are invaluable because the owner's address will be on the front if the  letter is to him, or on the back or in the upper left corner as a return address. A letter to someone else will at least reveal a person to contact who has some knowledge of the owner.

2. *Driver's License:* Tells you the owner's name, birth date, and current, or at least recent, address. If the information isn't current, the license number can help you track down the owner through the department of motor vehicles. Plus the photograph shows you what the owner looks like: including sex, race, and facial characteristics.

3. *Lists:* A shopping list or "to do" list can tell you a lot about the person who wrote it. If the list includes diapers or baby food, for example, you can deduce that the owner is either a parent of a small child or possibly works with babies or toddlers in a day-care center or hospital.

4. *Cards, Receipts, and Tickets:* A library card can tell you what city or town a person lives in. Receipts from stores may reveal the area in which a person lives or works, and the dates on the receipts indicate how recently the person has shopped there. Bus or train tickets show you the routes and dates a person has traveled. Other tickets—such as for movie theaters, ski areas, concerts, racetracks, or nightclubs—can tell you how a person spends his free time and where you might be likely to find him if he were a suspect or witness of a crime.

The Who's the Owner? Game

Do you think you have good deduction skills? Play this game and find out!

The leader asks a family member or friend if she can borrow an item of personal property such as a coat, purse, wallet, briefcase, or backpack. The owner should take out any valuable or private items but leave in any other clues such as the ones mentioned above. The leader also asks the lender for personal details—name, age, job/school, hobbies, interests, sports, family members, etc.—and enters these into his detective's notebook, then brings the item and her notes to the KDC meeting. The members

then divide up into two groups: Team A and Team B. The leader passes the object to Team A and gives the team members three minutes to deduce all they can about the owner of the object. When the time is up, Team A presents its list of deductions to the leader. Follow the same instructions for Team B. Once the leader has the lists from both teams, she compares them to the personal list she compiled and declares which team came closest to identifying and describing the owner of the object.

Helpful Hint

Clues can be deceptive. If you find a wallet on the street, you might assume that it belongs to a man. But many women use wallets, too! One of the most common mistakes a detective can make is to fail to look at the facts from different angles. Focusing on just one clue may lead you in the wrong direction. A good detective always keeps an open mind and double-checks the evidence and witness testimony.

Let Your Fingers Do the Walking

Taking Fingerprints

The ability to lift and compare fingerprints is one of the most important technical skills every detective needs to nab his suspect. That's because fingerprints are one of the few types of evidence that is considered 100-percent accurate in a court of law. Practice the activities in this chapter carefully, and you'll see how foolproof fingerprints are.

Create a Fingerprint File

The first step is to create a fingerprint file. This way, if you discover a crime, you'll be able to match the fingerprints you lift from the scene of the crime to those in your file and easily identify the culprit. Take a few blank sheets of white paper and your ink stamp pad, and follow these instructions:

1. Make sure your hands are clean and dry.

2. Open the ink pad and place it on a flat surface in front of you.

3. Lightly press one finger on the ink pad and roll it from side to side. The tip of your finger should be covered with ink. But be sure not to get too much ink on your fingertips, as this will make the print hard to read.

4. Press your index finger on a sheet of white paper. Roll your fingertip from one side to the other on the paper. Be careful not to roll back or you will blur the print.

5. Practice this a few times. When you are able to make clear prints, carefully enter a print of each of your fingers onto a sheet of paper, and label it with your name and the date.

6. Now ask your friends and family to put their prints in the file, too, so that you wind up with complete sets of their fingerprints, all neatly labeled. Keep your fingerprint file with the other materials in your kit as a handy reference.

Fingerprint Types

Use your magnifying glass to look at your prints. Hold it about an inch away from your eye and bring the print up to it. Move it around until you get the best view. The police group all fingerprints into eight types based on three basic patterns: *arches,* which are shaped like hills; *loops,* which have a single hairpin or upside-down *U* shape; and *whorls,* which go in circles or swirls. Here's what they look like:

ARCHES

Plain arch: shaped like a low, rounded hill

Tented arch: shaped like a high, pointed hill

WHORLS

Plain whorl: a pattern in circles or ovals

Central pocket loop: a whorl tucked inside a loop

LOOPS

Ulnar loop: slants toward the little finger side of the hand

Radial loop: slants toward the thumb side of the hand

Double loop: an *S* shape

Accidental whorl: a name for any other odd patterns that don't quite fit into the other whorl categories

Lifting Fingerprints

Now you need to learn how to lift fingerprints off an object. Empty your detective kit plastic case and handle it a lot and/or pass it around to your friends or family to make sure it's well fingerprinted. For the best prints, wash your hands, then wait five minutes. Just before you touch the object, rub your finger on the side of your nose or through your hair. It will pick up extra skin or hair oil and leave a better print. Touch the surface firmly, then lift your finger without sliding it across the surface. Now get out your pencil. Use scissors or a knife to scratch off a small pile of graphite powder into a saucer. Ask an adult to help you.

Use your paintbrush to very gently brush the powder over the outside surface of the box. You'll be surprised how many marks appear that were invisible before! A lot of those marks will look like blurry smudges at first. But when you examine them under your magnifying glass, you should find fingerprints.

Once a print has appeared, you can make it sharper by very gently working over and around it with the brush to clear away any extra powder. A print is called "sharp" when you can begin to count ridges—the tiny lines on it—without straining your eyes.

At this stage, police experts would normally start photographing the print with a camera so they can send it to the police records department to compare it to the millions of fingerprints in their files. But a much simpler—and cheaper—method of keeping prints is to use a strip of

clear adhesive tape. Lay the tape across the powdered print, sticky side down. The print will transfer to the tape. If you hold the tape up to the light and look at it through your magnifying glass, you will find that the print will show up as clearly as any photograph!

If you put the "taped" print into a clues envelope as it is, however, the tape will stick to the inside of the envelope and the print will be lost. So take a second strip of tape and press it on top of the first (putting the sticky sides of both tapes together). Now you have the fingerprint neatly caught between two pieces of tape and can put it in an envelope with no risk of losing it. Try comparing this print to the prints in your file. Can you nail the culprit?

The best places to find fingerprints around the house or in school are on hard, shiny surfaces such as doorknobs, light switches, and mirrors. Cloth, paper, cardboard, and leather do not show fingerprints well. If you are trying to lift fingerprints from clear or light-colored objects, use graphite powder. For dark objects, chalk or talcum powder works better.

Why don't criminals just try to change their fingerprints? It's impossible. Some people have tried to have their patterns surgically removed but have still been caught because our fingerprint patterns extend all the way down our fingers. You would have to remove all the skin from your hand to get rid of your prints! That's why most professional crooks wear gloves while they commit their crimes.

The History of Fingerprints

For more than a thousand years, people have been using fingerprints to identify themselves. In China about A.D. 700, fingerprints were used as signatures on business contracts. In the late 1800s the first modern, scientific fingerprinting methods were developed, and in 1891  Argentina set up the first fingerprint file to identify criminals. Still, up until the early 1900s most criminal identification was based on a complicated series of measurements of bony parts of the body. But there were two major problems: (1) it wasn't infallible and (2) most criminals don't leave their bones at the scene of the crime! The effectiveness of fingerprints was proved in 1903, when two prisoners at Leavenworth Prison who had the same name, same set of measurements, and the same appearance were found to have completely different fingerprints. Around that time, Britain's Sir Edward Henry, head of Scotland Yard, developed a fingerprint system, dubbed "The Henry System," which is still used all over the world today. Now the FBI's files contain between one and two billion fingerprints. It is such an effective tool because no two fingertip patterns are alike — not even those of identical twins! You were born with the exact same fingerprint patterns you have now; even as you get bigger, their distinctive shapes and patterns never change.

The Who Stole the Cookie? Game

Take a plate, and wipe it carefully with a towel. Put a cookie on it, then place it on a table in the middle of the room. Choose a member of the club to be the Detective and send him out of the room but within hearing distance. The remaining members choose someone to be the Crook. Then follow these simple instructions:

1. The Crook picks up the plate, then steals the cookie and conceals it.

2. The others shout, "Stop, thief!" but otherwise, nobody moves or speaks.

3. The Crook puts down the plate and quickly joins the crowd.

4. The Detective, having heard the shout, rushes back into the room.

5. He picks up the plate and, with the help of the finger-print powder, paintbrush, magnifying glass, and tape tries to find and lift the Crook's fingerprints.

6. The Detective then has to compare the fingerprints with the others in the club's fingerprint file and decide which member of the club is the Crook.

7. The Detective should be given a time limit—about ten minutes—to complete his investigation and announce his suspect. If he gets it right, he gets to eat the cookie!

Sealed with a Kiss

Surprise! Fingerprints aren't the only prints that give you away. Most people's lips have parts of at least two of the patterns below:

Short vertical grooves

Long vertical grooves

Rectangular grooves

Diamond grooves

Branching grooves

Making lip prints is easy. Ask your mother or older sister if you can borrow a tube of dark lipstick, or buy a cheap tube from a drugstore. Apply the lipstick on your lips, and rub your lips together to make sure the color is spread evenly. Then fold a sheet of white paper, put it between your lips, and press your lips firmly together. Be sure to open your mouth before removing the paper so you don't smudge the print. Have each member of your KDC make a lip print onto a drinking glass, then mix them up and see if you can identify one another's puckers!

Even certain animals can be identified by prints of different parts of their bodies! Monkeys and apes have fingerprints. Dogs have individual nose and paw prints. And horses have calluses called "chestnuts" on the inner side of their legs that are used for horse identification.

Fragile: Handle with Care!

Fingerprints and lip prints are, of course, only one of many kinds of clues that detectives use to solve crimes. Remember, no matter how big or small a clue is—whether it's a foot-square tracing of a bicycle tire track or a microscopic bit of fluff from a blanket—you must treat it very carefully! What if you found the torn half of a bus ticket under a desk and, for some reason, you thought it was an important clue? If you put that ticket into the back pocket of your jeans, for example, any possible fingerprints on it would be rubbed off immediately. And if you just shoved it into your wallet, it could easily get mixed up with all the other things you've got in there and end up battered, torn, or lost. So when you find a clue, be sure to follow these four steps:

1. Examine it with your magnifying glass and make sure it really is important.

2. Pick it up with a pair of tweezers so you don't get your own fingerprints on it.

3. Slip it into an envelope.

4. Write on the outside of the envelope the spot where it was found, the time at which you found it, and the date.

Bus Ticket
Found under John's desk
November 16 - 3:00

Practice spotting and collecting clues a few times around your house and then you can play detective games with your club.

Cookies

Whodunit?

Games to Practice Your Detecting Skills

The Careless Crook Game

This game begins like the Who Stole the Cookie? Game. Choose someone to be the Detective and send her out of the room. Then the remaining members of the club pick someone to be the Crook. Next choose a certain area of the room to be the Scene of the Crime, and draw marks with your chalk all around it. This shouldn't be a very big area—use your ruler to measure it and keep it to four feet square at the most. That's about enough room to fit a school desk and the chair behind it.

While all the other members of the club stand and watch, the Crook then has to leave five clues in the Scene of the Crime area. The clues must all be different. (Fingerprints, even if the Crook leaves them all over the place, still count as only one clue.) And each clue must be fair: In other words, it must be a reasonable pointer to the Crook's identity.

For example, suppose the Crook is a girl named Angela, that she has curly brown hair and is wearing a bright green sweater. She could leave:

1. Her fingerprints on top of the desk.

2. A strand of wool from her sweater on the seat of the chair.

3. A couple of strands of her hair inside the desk.

4. A gum wrapper on the floor beside the chair.

5. The top of her ballpoint pen underneath the chair.

She then asks if the other members of the club think these clues are fair. The club would agree that they are fair, provided that: Angela's ballpoint pen isn't exactly the same as anyone else's in the class and Angela is known to be a gum chewer. Otherwise, the club could insist that Angela leave a stronger clue—say a charm bracelet with an *A* on it or a comb.

Once the club has decided that five fair clues have been left, Angela leaves the Scene of the Crime area and becomes a seemingly innocent bystander, and the Detective is called back into the room.

She is shown the Scene of the Crime area and is allowed five minutes to go over it with a magnifying glass, flashlight, fingerprint powder—any item in the kit. At the end of ten minutes, the Detective has to name the Crook.

The Telltale Footprint Game

This game can be played on any stretch of concrete, but not, of course, on a road. In this game, the Detective should walk fifty or sixty paces away from the rest, preferably around a corner. And the Crook, instead of leaving fingerprints, leaves *footprints*. Here's how:

As soon as the Detective has left and the Crook has been chosen, the object to be stolen—say a football or a baseball bat—is placed in the middle of the concrete area. Everyone then wets the soles of his shoes—if it's been raining, by stepping into a shallow puddle; if it's dry, by pouring some water on the concrete and walking over the wet patch. (It's not just the Crook who wets his shoes because otherwise, the returning Detective would immediately spot who'd done it—he'd only have to look and see who had wet shoes!)

The members of the club form a circle around the object. The Crook then has to walk across and snatch it, leaving footprints all the way. As in the Who Stole the Cookie? Game, the others yell "Stop, thief!" The Crook then drops the object and runs to join the others before the Detective's return. (Everyone should shuffle around at this point or else the wet footprints will lead straight to the Crook.)

The Detective then has ten minutes to examine the footprints through his magnifying glass, measure them with his ruler, or whatever he wants to do with them. During this time, the Detective can ask club members to lift up their feet—one at a time, of course—and allow him to examine the soles and heels of their shoes. The Detective can take measurements of soles and heels but is not allowed to remove anyone's shoe. When the ten minutes are up, the Detective has to name the Crook.

Helpful Hint Shoes have all different kinds of patterned treads on their soles. Try to match up the ridges, bumps, or lines that you see in the print with the patterns on the bottom of the members' shoes. Also, sometimes the brand name of the manufacturer is stamped on the bottom of the shoe—if you're lucky, the print will clearly read *Reebok, Keds,* or some such and you'll be able to nail the Crook in a flash!

The Secret Formula Game

Choose a member of the club to be the Spy. Everyone leaves the room except the Spy—a special agent who has been given an extremely tough assignment. Although she is trapped in a room with all those enemies outside the door, she has in her possession a vitally important secret formula:

$$A + B = 333$$

She knows that sometime soon a fellow agent will be along this way, and it is her job to leave the formula hidden in the room where her enemies won't spot it but where her fellow agent will.

She can scrawl the formula on a piece of paper and leave it tucked between two floorboards or crumpled up in the top of a ballpoint pen left casually on a desk. She can scribble it on a candy wrapper and chuck it in the wastebasket. She can pencil it on the inside rim of a plant pot in the corner. Basically, she can hide it anywhere except in her clothes or on her person. And she may not hide it in anyone else's personal property, such as the inside of a locker or a desk.

The Spy should be allowed three minutes alone in the room to hide the formula, and the rest of the club—the Spy Catchers—are allowed five minutes in which to find it. This game will prove whether you have what it takes to be a secret agent: brains, speed, and an ability to work under pressure!

Mini-Mystery

Gather your KDC members, set your timer for five minutes, and see who can solve this mystery:

A police officer, Officer Mitchell, is driving down the road when she gets an emergency call—a robbery has been reported at Joe's Hardware Store in the mall on Main Street. Officer Mitchell rushes to the scene and spots two people getting into their cars in the parking lot near the hardware store. She stops them both and questions them about the crime. The driver of the first car jumps out, points to the driver of the other car, and says, "She did it! I saw the whole thing! She just pulled right in here, ran into Joe's Hardware, and ran out!" The driver of the second car looks startled and says, "I—I don't know what you're talking about. I didn't do anything. I've been at my aerobics class for an hour, and then I shopped for a while in the mall." Officer Mitchell looks at them both carefully, then says, "Thank you, that's all the information I need. Now please just sit here while I figure this out."

How will Officer Mitchell figure out who is telling the truth and who is the culprit?

Answer: Officer Mitchell will touch the motor on both cars. The second suspect says her car has been parked at the mall for over an hour. If that's true, her motor should be cool. If it is cool, then Officer Mitchell would wonder why the first suspect lied about what he saw. The most likely reason is that he is the culprit himself and is trying to cover up his crime.

Hands Up!

Identifying Handwriting

You've probably noticed in the movies or on television that anonymous ransom notes and death threats are often created by cutting up letters from a magazine or newspaper and pasting them together into a message.

Why do criminals take the time to do this? Wouldn't it be easier to just write the letter by hand? Expert detectives can tell you why: It is almost impossible to disguise your handwriting. Try to copy someone else's signature. See how hard it is to make it look natural? Remember, everyone's handwriting is as unique as his fingerprints, and the peculiarities aren't hard to spot!

Here are some tips for identifying handwriting.

Write this sentence on a piece of paper:

The shy brown fox jumped quickly over the lazy dog.

1. Notice how you make particular letters. Do your *T*'s have a special curl on the top? Do you use capital style *A*'s even when you're writing in lower case? Even if you are trying to disguise your handwriting, it will be hard for you to change these habits because you probably do them unconsciously.

2. Analyze how the letters are joined together. Are they spaced apart or crowded together? Do they slant to the left or right or are they straight up and down?

3. Draw four lines through your sentence, as shown. Examine how the letters fit within each zone.

Top Zone ⟶
Middle Zone ⟶ *shy brown fox*
Lower Zone ⟶

The Name Game

Choose a Detective, and have him leave the room. Each member of the club should write their full name on a piece of paper. Then choose one member to write a mystery note, such as "Beware the West Side Gang!" The Detective returns to the room and, using the tips above, tries to identify the note writer by his handwriting. He has three minutes to finger the culprit.

Did you know you can't tell a woman's handwriting from a man's? Not even the world's greatest handwriting experts can do it!

Spot a Counterfeit Bill

Have you ever been at a store or bank and seen the clerk hold a bill up to the light? About ten million dollars in counterfeit, or fake, money is made and circulated each year, and many people who handle a lot of money are trained to identify it. Use your magnifying glass to look at a one, five, ten, or twenty dollar bill—can you spot a fake?

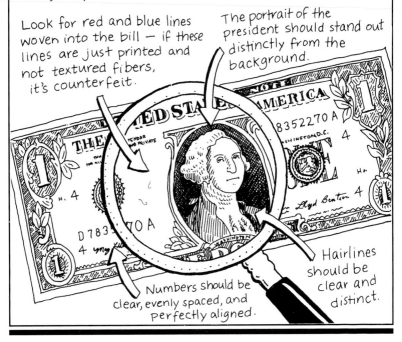

Look for red and blue lines woven into the bill — if these lines are just printed and not textured fibers, it's counterfeit.

The portrait of the president should stand out distinctly from the background.

Numbers should be clear, evenly spaced, and perfectly aligned.

Hairlines should be clear and distinct.

Special Delivery

Sending Secret Messages

Even though you can't disguise *how* you write, you can disguise *what* you write. Say you want to send a note to let a club member know about a top secret meeting, but you're worried about nonmembers eavesdropping or intercepting your note. Here are three ways you can send a secret message and ensure that only you and your fellow super-sleuths will be able to read and understand your note.

Compose a "Hidden Message" Letter

Pick a number that appears in your return address. Make it clear to the receiver that this is your "key" by underlining it. This number tells the reader that she can decipher the message inside by counting out the words in the letter until she reaches that number and then piecing together all the words to create a new message. Try finding the hidden message in the letter shown on the next page.

41

73 Chestnut Street
Boston, Massachusetts 02106

Dear Jill,
It was really great to see you
yesterday. But I bet you are like
me today — feeling under the
weather after Aunt Lizzie's cherry
pie! I know I ate tree pieces. I'm
sure you had at least as many.
Maybe even four! Hope we're
both okay by Wednesday.
                    Love,
                    Angela

Answer: SEE YOU UNDER CHERRY TREE AT FOUR WEDNESDAY.

Write in Invisible Ink

Did you know you probably already have a bottle of invisible ink in your house? Just look in the kitchen! Milk, lemon juice, or white vinegar will make excellent invisible ink. Pour a little of one of these liquids into a jar or glass. Dip the plastic tip (not the brush end) of your paintbrush into the liquid, and write your message on a piece of blank paper. Dip your writing instrument into the liquid frequently to make sure you're using enough ink. After the ink has dried (note: milk takes over an hour to dry; lemon juice and vinegar should dry in a few minutes), deliver it to one of your fellow super-sleuths. The receiver should ask an adult to help him heat the paper above a candle flame, over the heating element of a kitchen stove, or even against a hot radiator. Hold the paper far enough away from the heat source so that it becomes warm but not hot (and be careful not to burn it!) Soon, the message will come up in bright brownish-yellowish letters!

Create a Secret Code

On a sheet of blank paper, write down the entire alphabet. Then write down a second alphabet underneath the first

—but not exactly underneath it: Move your second alphabet one or more spaces along to the left. The positioning of the second alphabet against the first gives you the code. Take a look at the code below:

```
A B C D E F G H I J K L M N O P Q R S T U V W X Y Z
A B C D E F G H I J K L M N O P Q R S T U V W X Y Z A B C
```

(Note: after *Z* on the second row, you start the alphabet again.)

With this diagram in front of you, you can put together a secret message in minutes! Just switch each letter for its "code" letter below it. Instead of *A*, you write *D*. Instead of *B*, you write *E*. Instead of *K*, you write *N*. And so on all the way to *Z* (which now becomes *C*). Suppose you wanted to write: THE PASSWORD IS NOW "BLACK CAT." The coded message would read: WKH SDVVZRUG LV QRZ "EODFN FDW." Easy, isn't it? Practice by trying to decode the following three secret messages, using the code above:

WKH NHB LV LQ WKH JDUDJH.
PHHW MH WKH FOXELRXVH DW WZR.
LHOS! VSPHRQH MV IROORZMQ PH.

If you were able to crack these codes, you're ready to make up some of your own!

Morse Code

Probably the most famous code in the world is Morse code. Named after Samuel F. B. Morse, this code has been the standby of secret agents ever since it was invented in 1832. Originally used to transmit messages by telegraph, it has been tapped on the walls of innumerable prison cells; lights have flashed it up to planes; whistles and foghorns have blasted it across the seas; it has even been sent by waving flags. During World War II, the famous Victory *V* (dot dot dot dash) was drummed

Samuel F.B. Morse

endlessly over the air by the BBC in England to encourage the Resistance movements in Europe.

But this code isn't just for armies and spies; anyone can use it. Dots are tapped rapidly and dashes more slowly, with a short pause afterward. Between letters, make a slightly longer pause, and a longer pause between words. After a day of serious practice, you can tap out messages on a bathroom stall, bedroom wall, or flash them with a flashlight or lamp to your neighbor across the street!

Here it is:

A · −	H · · · ·	O − − −	V · · · −
B − · · ·	I · ·	P · − − ·	W · − −
C − · − ·	J · − − −	Q − − · −	X − · · −
D − · ·	K − · −	R · − ·	Y − · − −
E ·	L · − · ·	S · · ·	Z − − · ·
F · · − ·	M − −	T −	
G − − ·	N − ·	U · · −	

Can you figure out how to send an S.O.S. signal in Morse code?

Fun Fact

Morse code might be the most famous code, but one of the most clever—and successful—ones was created by the Navajo Indians. During World War II, the United States Marines sometimes sent secret military messages via the Navajos, who communicated in their native language over the radio. The Japanese were never able to decipher this unique system!

The Perfect Crime

Putting Your Detecting Skills to Work

Now that you've learned all the fundamentals of crime investigation, it's time for you to put them to use.

Conduct an Investigation

Get together the members of your club to plot out the perfect crime and see if the Detective can solve it. Tear up a piece of paper into small strips—as many pieces as there are members of your club. Write the word *Suspect* on all the pieces except two. The last two pieces of paper each have one word on them: *Detective* and *Crook.* Put them all in a hat or a bag.

Each member draws a piece of paper out of the hat and reads what is written on it. Then everyone except the Detective folds up his piece of paper and pockets it without letting anyone else see it. The Detective shows his piece of paper to everyone to prove that he has been selected as the Detective. In other words, throughout the game, everyone knows who the Detective is, but no one knows who the Crook is—except, of course, the Crook.

And the Suspects are not allowed to tell one another, or the Detective, what they are.

Next, the Detective names a certain object in his possession, which he challenges the Crook to steal within the next twenty-four hours. The object must be something reasonably portable and inexpensive, such as a book or a T-shirt. The Detective is not allowed to carry it on his person, and it has to be in a reasonably accessible place—for example, his yard, backpack, school desk, or bike saddle-bag—and it cannot be protected by a lock. Nor can the Detective take any special steps to guard it. (The Crook needs to have a reasonable chance.)

The Crook is also restricted. He is not allowed to tell any of the Suspects who he is or to use any of them as accomplices. And he is not allowed to wear gloves.

(It's possible that if the Crook is clumsy, he might be caught red-handed by the Detective, in the act of stealing the object. In this case, you should start the game over.)

Once the Crook has succeeded in stealing the object, the Detective has twenty-four hours in which to investigate the crime and name the Crook.

Keep in mind the following rules:

- No Suspect can refuse to be questioned by the Detective, and they must all tell the truth. Only the Crook is allowed to lie.

- The Suspects must allow the Detective to search any of their belongings at any time and to take their fingerprints. And so, of course, must the Crook—if he doesn't want to give himself away!

- The Detective is not allowed to question anyone who is not in the game.

- The Detective is allowed to search all the suspects only once—immediately after he discovers the crime has taken place.

The Detective then gets out his scene-of-the-crime kit and begins his investigation, following these steps:

1. *Examining the scene of the crime and collecting clues:* Decide which surfaces the Crook is most likely to have touched, and try to get fingerprints. Look for stray hairs, cloth fibers or tiny bits of fabric, and any objects that might have fallen from the culprit's pockets. Place each clue in a separate envelope, and label it.

2. *Search the Suspects:* This is called "frisking" by police. Get the Suspect to face a wall. He should bend forward with his face down and his hands flat against the wall so he can't attack you. Starting with the ankles, quickly pat all the way up his sides and arms. Check his pockets as well as anywhere else he may have hidden the object —such as under a hat, in his gloves, or in his shoes.

3. *Interview the Suspects:* Meet with each Suspect individually so none of them can hear what the other Suspects say. Find out where each Suspect was at the time of the crime. Check to see if their alibis (the defense of having been somewhere else when a crime was committed) match.

4. *Crack your case:* If you analyze your clues carefully, read your notes repeatedly, and make wise deductions, within twenty-four hours you should be able to name your prime Suspect, as well as the approximate time the object was stolen.

Congratulations! You've got what it takes to be a first-class sleuth!

Tips for a Successful Interview

- Try to put the person you are interviewing at ease. Be polite and thank her for her time and help. Remember, if the suspect is nervous, she'll be more likely to lie—even if she's not guilty!

- Prepare your questions ahead of time in writing.

- Ask short, concise questions, such as "What were you doing on Monday afternoon around 2:30?" so that you get clear answers.

- If you sense the person is lying, keep asking the same question a different way to see if you can catch her in a lie.

- Try to keep a blank face so the suspect doesn't know what you're thinking.

Thieves find all kinds of ways to hide their stolen loot. Watch out for these suspicious signs:

Wearing shoes that are too big

Fake bandages or slings

Wearing a coat all buttoned up on a hot day

Bumps and bulges under a coat

Empty baby carriages, grocery bags, or suitcases

Sometimes when police departments or private detectives are stuck on a case, they hire professional psychics to aid them in finding clues. A psychic is someone with an extraordinary ability to "see" into the past and future. Not everyone believes in them, but many psychics have played an important part in solving mysterious crimes. In one case, a detective asked a psychic to help him track down a missing girl. After she was brought to a semi-hypnotic state by a doctor, the psychic visualized a house with a red door with the numbers 1 and 6 on it. She also thought the street might have a president's name and that taxis were involved in some way. Using this information, the detective drove around town and soon discovered the girl at 186 Monroe Street in a house with an office that operated a taxi dispatching service.

Stop Right There!

Some Crime Prevention Tips

After learning all these detective skills, it would be pretty embarrassing if someone were able to commit a crime right under your nose, wouldn't it? You can take steps to prevent crime from happening to you by following a few simple rules:

1. Lock up any personal belongings that you can, and don't ever lend your key or tell your combination number to anyone. Don't write your combination number down—a thief might find it! Be sure to memorize it instead.

2. Don't leave valuable items (such as a camera, calculator, or watch) out in plain view. It will only tempt someone to steal it.

3. Never leave dollar bills in your back pocket. They can easily work their way up and out. Keep them in a purse or wallet or at least in your front pocket, where it would be difficult for someone to take something without you noticing.

4. Keep an inventory of important personal items with a detailed description of each so that if something *is* stolen, you will be able to give the police the most accurate description possible.

Sample Personal Inventory

Item	Brand	Model	Size	Color	Peculiarities
Walkman	Sony	3-364-643-01	3" wide x4½" long	black	Red Sox sticker on front

*Note: Most items also have a serial number on them somewhere. On bikes, it's usually under the crankset, where the pedals are (turn your bike upside-down to find it). On a radio, it's usually stamped on the back of the set or in the battery compartment. It might be hard to find, but try to keep a record of it if possible (remember to ask the dealer when you buy the item or ask your parents to help you locate it)—it may be the key clue that gets your item back if it's stolen.

How to Set a Trap

Do you suspect anyone of trying to steal something from you? Maybe your little brother has been borrowing your favorite comic books or new cassettes without your permission. Here are some tricks that will help you catch him in the act:

1. Close your bedroom door and stick a paper clip in the hinge. It will fall down if anyone opens the door.

2. Leave a book open at a particular page and see if it's moved.

3. Open each drawer of your dresser or desk a different amount and check to see if the positions change.

4. Sprinkle a little baby powder in front of your door to catch any footprints.

5. Keep track of how your books or cassettes are arranged on your shelf, and see if they appear out of order.

54

6. Sprinkle breakfast cereal around your floor. This will make a crunching sound if the thief tries to creep into your room at night.

CRUNCH!

Make Your Own Burglar Alarm

Find a few empty tin cans (make sure there are no jagged edges so you won't cut yourself) and fill them with a  handful of marbles, rocks, or dried beans—anything that makes a sound. Tie a string around each one for a handle. Then hang one off your doorknob, one from your window latch—anywhere a thief might infiltrate. The loud rattling sound the alarm makes when the door or window is opened will alert you to trouble as effectively as any professional burglar alarm!

How to Report a Real Crime to the Police

If you witness a crime in progress or suspect one is about to happen, the best thing to do is to ask your parents or another adult to call the police. But if you're far from home and you believe a crime is about to be committed very soon, then you should call the police yourself from a pay phone. (It's a good idea to always have some dimes and quarters in your pocket for this purpose.) You'll find the number in the phone book under *P* for Police. Or in a real emergency (say you've seen some vandals smashing a shop window or heard someone yell for help), you can simply pick up the receiver and dial 911 or *O* for Operator. Just ask for the police and you'll be connected right away. Don't be shy! If the story is serious and you have exact details to offer, the police will be grateful for your help.

This is the kind of information that would be most helpful to a real detective investigating a possible crime:

1. **The time:** Try to wear a watch at all times, and write down the exact time the suspicious activity occurred (9:35 A.M., 2:11 P.M., or whatever).

2. **The place:** Don't just put the name of the street but also the number of the nearest house or the name of the nearest store or recognizable building—anything that will identify the exact spot you mean.

3. **The car:** If a car is involved, note the make, color, and license plate number as well as anything noticeable such as dents, scratches, or bumper stickers.

4. The suspect(s): Write down a quick description that includes things such as *height, build, color of eyes, color and style of hair, complexion, clothing,* and *special features.*

Write Away!

Did you know that more than 35 million crimes are committed in the United States alone each year? A good detective is devoted to fighting crime and protecting the public. If you care about crime, let someone important know. Try writing to a government leader, such as the head of your local police department, your mayor, governor, or the president. Here is a sample letter you can use as a guideline:

(name and address of person you are writing to)

(date)

Dear *(name)*,

   I am in a kid detectives club, and I am writing to you because I am concerned about crime in my neighborhood/city/country. I think we should all be working to make the streets safer for everyone.

   I would like to hear what you are doing to fight crime. I would also like to know your ideas about how kids can help.

   I hope to hear from you soon. Thank you.

Sincerely,

(your signature)

(your name & address, printed clearly)

Here are some important addresses:

The President, The White House, 1600 Pennsylvania Avenue NW, Washington, D.C. 20500

The Prime Minister, House of Commons, Ottawa, Ontario, Canada K1A 0A2

The Prime Minister, 10 Downing Street, London SW1A 2AA, England

A parent, teacher, or librarian can help you find addresses for local officials.

Case Closed

A Final Word about Becoming a Real-Life Detective

Any professional detective will tell you that your success in investigating crime is determined by a combination of training, creativity, common sense, and luck. But how do you get to become a professional detective in the first place? Here are a few things you should know. First of all, there are two kinds:

1. *Police detectives* are hired by the state to protect the community. They investigate crimes reported to the police, such as robberies and murders, with the intent of obtaining information that can lead to a conviction of the perpetrators. To become a detective in the police department, you must start out as a police officer and work your way up to being promoted to detective by developing your powers of observation and deduction on the job.

2. *Private investigators* (P.I.'s) are usually hired by private clients; they investigate crimes with the intent of providing information for those clients, who may or may not choose to take legal action. They are often hired, for example, to track down missing persons or collect information regarding debtors (people who owe money to other people or businesses). To become a P.I., you must complete an apprenticeship with a licensed P.I., usually for a period of two to three years.

Either way, you must be at least twenty-five years old to qualify and are required to pass a test, after which you receive a certificate and a pocket identification card that proves you are a licensed detective. So, if you think you might want to be a real detective when you grow up, your best bet is to practice all the skills in this book—that way you'll have a head start!